STEALER OF SOULS

DIANA WYNNE JONES was born in August 1934 in London, where she had a chaotic and unsettled childhood against the background of World War II. The family moved around a lot, finally settling in rural Essex. As children, Diana and her two sisters were deprived of a steady supply of books by a father, "who could beat Scrooge in a meanness contest". So, armed with a vivid imagination and an insatiable appetite for stories, she decided that she would have to write them herself.

Her first book was published in 1973 and since then she has written over 40 books. When writing, she is totally absorbed in the work and on one never-to-be forgotten occasion, her sons returned from school ravenous to find she had shoved a pair of muddy shoes in the oven for their tea!

Charmed Life won the 1997 Guardian Award for Children's Books, and Diana's books continue to enthral readers all over the world. She was runner-up for the Children's Book Award in 1981, and twice runner-up for the Carnegie Medal. In 1999, she won the children's section of the Mythopeic Award in the USA, and the Karl Edward Wagner Award in the UK – which is awarded by the British Fantasy Society to individuals or organisations who have made a significant impact on fantasy.

Other titles by Diana Wynne Jones

Chrestomanci Series
Charmed Life*
The Magicians of Caprona*
Witch Week*
The Lives of Christopher Chant*
Mixed Magics

Black Maria*
A Tale of Time City
Howl's Moving Castle*
Castle in the Air*
The Homeward Bounders
Archer's Goon*
Dogsbody
Eight Days of Luke
Wilkins' Tooth

For older readers
Fire and Hemlock
Hexwood
The Time of the Ghost

For younger readers
Wild Robert
Stopping for a Spell

* *also available on tape*

STEALER OF SOULS
BY
DianaWynneJones

Illustrated by Tim Stevens

An imprint of HarperCollinsPublishers

Stealer of Souls was first published in *Mixed Magics*, Collins 2000
This edition published for World Book Day by CollinsVoyager 2002

CollinsVoyager is an imprint of HarperCollins*Publishers* Ltd
77-85 Fulham Palace Road, Hammersmith,
London, W6 8JB

The HarperCollins website address is:
www.**fire**and**water**.com

1 3 5 7 9 8 6 4 2

Stealer of Souls © Diana Wynne Jones 2000

Illustrations by Tim Stevens 2000

ISBN 0 00 714270-6

The author and illustrator assert the moral right to be
identified as the author and illustrator of the work.

Printed and bound in Great Britain by
Omnia Books Limited, Glasgow

There are thousands of worlds, all different from ours. Chrestomanci's world is the one next door to us, and the difference here is that magic is as common as music is with us. It is full of people working magic – warlocks, witches, thaumaturges, sorcerers, fakirs, conjurors, hexers, magicians, mages, shamans, diviners and many more – from the lowest Certified Witch right up to the most powerful of enchanters. Enchanters are strange as well as powerful. Their magic is different and stronger and many of them have more than one life.

Now, if someone did not control all these busy magic-users, ordinary people would have a horrible time and probably end up as slaves. So the government appoints the very strongest enchanter there is to make sure no one misuses magic. This enchanter has nine lives and is known as 'the Chrestomanci'. You pronounce it KREST-OH-MAN-SEE. He has to have a strong personality as well as strong magic.

Diana Wynne Jones

Cat Chant was not altogether happy, either with himself or with other people. The reason was the Italian boy that Chrestomanci had unexpectedly brought back to Chrestomanci Castle after his trip to Italy.

"Cat," said Chrestomanci, who was looking rather tired after his travels, "this is Antonio Montana. You'll find he has some very interesting magic."

Cat looked at the Italian boy, and the Italian boy held out his hand and said, "How do you do. Please call me Tonino," in excellent English, but with a slight halt at the end of each word, as if he was used to words that mostly ended in 'o'. Cat knew at that instant that he was going to count the days until someone took Tonino back to Italy again. And he hoped someone would do it soon.

It was not just the beautiful English and the good manners. Tonino had fair hair – that almost greyish fair hair people usually call ash blond – which Cat had never imagined an Italian could have. It looked very sophisticated and it made Cat's hair look a crude straw colour by comparison. As if this was not enough, Tonino had trusting brown eyes and a nervous expression, and he was evidently younger than Cat. He looked so sweet that Cat shook hands as quickly as he could without being rude, knowing at once that everyone would expect him to look after Tonino.

"Pleased to meet you," he lied.

Sure enough, Chrestomanci said, "Cat, I'm sure I can trust you to show Tonino the ropes here and keep an eye on him until he finds his feet in England."

Cat sighed. He knew he was going to be very bored.

But it was worse than that. The other children in the castle thought Tonino was lovely. They all did their best to be friends with him. Chrestomanci's daughter Julia patiently taught Tonino all the games you played in England, including cricket. Chrestomanci's son Roger joined in the cricket lessons and then spent hours gravely comparing spells with Tonino. Chrestomanci's ward Janet spent further hours enthusiastically asking Tonino about Italy. Janet came from another world where Italy was quite different, and she was interested in the differences.

And yet, despite all this attention, Tonino went around with a lost, lonely look which made Cat avoid him. He could tell Tonino was acutely homesick. In fact, Cat was fairly sure Tonino was feeling just like Cat had felt himself when he first came to Chrestomanci Castle, and Cat could not get over the annoyance of having someone have feelings that were *his*. He knew this was stupid – this was partly why he was not happy with himself – but he was not happy with Julia, Roger and Janet either. He considered that they were making a stupid fuss over Tonino. The fact was that Julia and Roger normally looked after Cat. He had grown used to being the youngest and unhappiest person in the castle, until Tonino had come along and stolen his thunder. Cat knew all this perfectly well, but it did not make the slightest difference to the way he felt.

To make things worse, Chrestomanci himself was extremely interested in Tonino's magic. He spent large parts of the next few days with Tonino doing experiments to discover just what the extent of Tonino's powers was, while Cat, who was used to being the one with the interesting magic, was left to wrestle with problems of Magic Theory by himself in Chrestomanci's study.

"Tonino," Chrestomanci said, by way of explanation, "can, it seems, not only reinforce other people's spells, but also make use of any magic other people do. If it's true, it's a highly unusual ability. And by the way," he added, turning round in the doorway, looking tall enough to brush the ceiling, "you don't seem to have shown Tonino round the castle yet. How come?"

"I was busy – I forgot," Cat muttered sulkily.

"Fit it into your crowded schedule soon, please," Chrestomanci said, "or I may find myself becoming seriously irritated."

Cat sighed, but nodded. No one disobeyed Chrestomanci when he got like this. But now he had to face the fact that Chrestomanci knew exactly how Cat was feeling and had absolutely no patience with it. Cat sighed again as he got down to his problems.

Magic Theory left him completely bewildered. His trouble was that he could, instinctively, do magic that used very advanced Magic Theory indeed, and he had no idea how he did it. Sometimes he did not even know he was doing magic. Chrestomanci said Cat *must* learn Theory or he might one day do something quite terrible by mistake. As far as Cat was concerned, the one thing he wanted magic to do was to solve Theory problems, and that seemed to be the one thing you couldn't use it for.

He got six answers he knew were nonsense. Then, feeling very neglected and put-upon, he took Tonino on a tour of the castle. It was not a success. Tonino looked white and tired and timid almost the whole time, and shivered in the long cold passages and on all the dark chilly staircases. Cat could not think of anything to say except utterly obvious things like, "This is called the Small Drawing Room," or, "This is the schoolroom – we have lessons here with Michael Saunders,

10

but he's away in Greenland just now," or, "Here's the front hall – it's made of marble."

The only time Tonino showed the slightest interest was when they came to the big windows that overlooked the velvety green lawn and the great cedars of the gardens. He actually hooked a knee on the windowsill to look down at it.

"My mother has told me of this," he said, "but I never thought it would be so wet and green."

"How does your mother know about the gardens?" Cat asked.

"She is English. She was brought up here in this castle when Gabriel de Witt, who was Chrestomanci before this one, collected many children with magic talents to be trained here," Tonino replied.

Cat felt annoyed and somehow cheated that Tonino had a connection with the castle anyway. "Then you're English too," he said. It came out as if he were accusing Tonino of a crime.

"No, I am Italian," Tonino said firmly. He added, with great pride, "I belong to the foremost spell-house in Italy."

There did not seem to be any reply to this. Cat did think of saying, "And I'm going to be the next Chrestomanci – I've got nine lives, you know," but he knew this would be silly and boastful. Tonino had not been boasting really. He had been trying to say why he did not belong in the castle. So Cat simply took Tonino back to the playroom, where Julia was only too ready to teach him card games, and mooched away, feeling he had done his duty. He tried to avoid Tonino after that. He did not like being made to feel the way Tonino made him feel.

Unfortunately, Julia went down with measles the next day,

and Roger the day after that. Cat had had measles long before he came to the castle, and so had Tonino. Janet could not remember whether she had had them or not, although she assured them that there was measles in the world she came from, because you could be injected against it. "Maybe I've been injected," she suggested hopefully.

Chrestomanci's wife Millie gave Janet a worried look. "I think you'd better stay away from Roger and Julia all the same," she said.

"But you're an enchantress," Janet said. "You could stop me getting them."

"Magic has almost no effect on measles," Millie told her. "I wish it did, but it doesn't. Cat can see Roger and Julia if he wants, but you keep away."

Cat went to Roger's bedroom and then Julia's and was shocked at how ill they both were. He could see it was going to be weeks before they were well enough to look after Tonino. He found himself, quite urgently and cold-bloodedly (and in spite of what Millie had said) putting a spell on Janet to make sure she did not go down with measles too. He knew as he did it that it was probably the most selfish thing he had ever done, but he simply could not bear to be the only one left to look after Tonino. By the time he got back to the schoolroom, he was in a very bad mood.

"How are they?" Janet asked him anxiously.

"Awful," Cat said out of his bad mood. "Roger's sort of purple and Julia's uglier than ever."

"Do you think Julia's ugly then?" Janet said. "I mean, in the normal way."

"Yes," said Cat. "Plump and pudgy, like you said."

"I was angry when I told you that and being unfair," said Janet. "You shouldn't believe me when I'm angry, Cat. I'll take a bet with you, if you like, that Julia grows up a raving beauty, as good-looking as her father. She's got his bones to her face. And, you must admit, Chrestomanci is taller and darker and handsomer than any man has any right to be!"

She kept giving little dry coughs as she spoke. Cat examined her with concern. Janet's extremely pretty face showed no sign of any spots, but her golden hair was hanging in lifeless hanks and her big blue eyes were slightly red about the rims. He suspected that he had been too late with his spell. "And Roger?" he asked. "Is he going to grow up ravingly beautiful too?"

Janet looked dubious. "He takes after Millie. But," she added, coughing again, "he'll be very nice."

"Not like me then," Cat said sadly. "I'm nastier than everyone. I think I'm growing into an evil enchanter. And I think you've got measles too."

"I have *not*!" Janet exclaimed indignantly.

But she had. By that evening she was in bed too, freckled purple all over and looking uglier than Julia. The maids once again ran up and down stairs with possets to bring down fever, while Millie used the new telephone at the top of the marble stairs to ask the doctor to call again.

"I shall go mad," she told Cat. "Janet's really ill, worse than the other two. Go and make sure Tonino's not feeling too neglected, there's a good boy."

I knew it! Cat thought and went very slowly back to the playroom.

Behind him, the telephone rang again. He heard Millie answer it. He had gone three slow steps when he heard the telephone go back on its rest. Millie uttered a great groan and Chrestomanci at once came out of the office to see what was wrong. Cat prudently made himself invisible.

"Oh lord!" Millie said. "That was Mordecai Roberts. Why does everything happen at once? Gabriel de Witt wants to see Tonino tomorrow."

"That's awkward," Chrestomanci said. "Tomorrow I've got to be in Series One for the Conclave of Mages."

"But I really *must* stay here with the other children," Millie said. "Janet's going to need all magic can do for her, particularly for her eyes. Can we put Gabriel off?"

"I don't think so," Chrestomanci replied, unusually seriously. "Tomorrow could be Gabriel's last chance to see anyone. His lives are leaving him steadily now. And he was thrilled when I told him about Tonino. He's always hoped we'd find someone with back-up magic one day. I know what, though. We can send Cat with Tonino. Gabriel's almost equally interested in Cat, and the responsibility will do Cat good."

No it won't! Cat thought. I *hate* responsibility! As he fled invisibly back to the playroom, he thought Why *me*? Why can't they send one of the wizards on the staff, or Miss Bessemer, or someone? But of course everyone was going to be busy, with Chrestomanci away and Millie looking after Janet.

In the playroom, Tonino was curled up on one of the shabby sofas deep in one of Julia's favourite books. He barely looked up as the door seemed to open by itself and Cat shook himself visible again.

Tonino, Cat realised, was an avid reader. He knew the signs from Janet and Julia. That was a relief. Cat went quietly away to his own room and collected all the books there that Janet had been trying to make him read and that Cat had somehow not got round to – how could Janet expect him to read books called *Millie Goes to School* anyway? – and brought the whole armful back to the playroom.

"Here," he said, dumping them on the floor beside Tonino. "Janet says these are good."

And he thought, as he curled up on the other battered sofa, that this was exactly how a person got to be an evil enchanter, by doing a whole lot of good things for bad reasons. He tried to think of ways to get out of looking after Tonino tomorrow.

Cat always dreaded going to visit Gabriel de Witt anyway. He was so old-fashioned and sharp and so obviously an enchanter, and you had to remember to behave in an old-fashioned polite way all the time you were there. But these days it was worse than that. As Chrestomanci had said, old Gabriel's nine lives were leaving him one by one. Every time Cat was taken to see him, Gabriel de Witt looked iller and older and more gaunt, and Cat's secret dread was that one day he would be there, making polite conversation, and actually *see* one of Gabriel's lives as it went away. If he did, he knew he would scream.

The dread of this happening so haunted Cat that he could scarcely speak to Gabriel for watching and waiting for a life to leave. Gabriel de Witt told Chrestomanci that Cat was a strange, reserved boy. To which Chrestomanci answered "Really?" in his most sarcastic way.

People, Cat thought, should be looking after *him*, and not breaking his spirit by forcing him to take Italian boys to see elderly enchanters. But he could think of no way to get out of it that Millie or Chrestomanci would not see through at once. Chrestomanci seemed to know when Cat was being dishonest even before Cat knew it himself. Cat sighed and went to bed hoping that Chrestomanci would have changed his mind in the morning and decided to send someone else with Tonino.

This was not to be. At breakfast, Chrestomanci appeared (in a sea-green dressing gown with a design of waves breaking on it) to tell Cat and Tonino that they were catching the ten thirty train to Dulwich to visit Gabriel de Witt. Then he went away and Millie – who looked very tired from having sat up half the night with Janet – rustled in to give them their train fare.

Tonino frowned. "I do not understand. Was not Monsignor de Witt the former Chrestomanci, Lady Chant?"

"Call me Millie, please," said Millie. "Yes, that's right. Gabriel stayed in the post until he felt Christopher was ready to take over and then he retired – Oh, I see! You thought he was *dead*! Oh no, far from it. Gabriel's as lively and sharp as ever he was, you'll see."

There was a time when Cat had thought that the last Chrestomanci was dead too. He had thought that the present Chrestomanci had to die before the next one took over, and he used to watch this Chrestomanci rather anxiously in case Chrestomanci showed signs of losing his last two lives and thrusting Cat into all the huge responsibility of looking after the magic in this world. He had been quite relieved to find it was more normal than that.

"There's nothing to worry about," Millie said. "Mordecai Roberts is going to meet you at the station and then he'll take you back there in a cab after lunch. And Tom is going to drive you to the station here in the car and meet you off the three nineteen when you get back. Here's the money, Cat, and an extra five shillings in case you need a snack on the way back – because efficient as I *know* Miss Rosalie is, she doesn't have any idea how much boys need to eat. She never did have and she hasn't changed. And I want to hear all about it when you get home."

She gave them a warm hug each and rushed away, murmuring, "Lemon barley, febrifuge in half an hour, and then the eye-salve."

Tonino pushed away his cocoa. "I think I am ill on trains."

This proved to be true. Luckily Cat managed to get them a carriage to themselves after the young man who acted as Chrestomanci's secretary had dropped them at the station. Tonino sat at the far corner of the smoky little space, with the window pulled down as low as it would go and his handkerchief pressed to his mouth. Though he did not actually bring up his breakfast, he went whiter and whiter, until Cat could hardly credit that a person could be so pale.

"Were you like this all the way from Italy?" Cat asked him, slightly awed.

"Rather worse," Tonino said through the handkerchief, and swallowed desperately.

Cat knew he should sympathise. He got travel-sick himself, but only in cars. But instead of feeling sorry for Tonino, he did not know whether to feel superior or annoyed that Tonino, once again, was more to be pitied than *he* was.

At least it meant that Cat did not have to talk to him.

Dulwich was a pleasant village a little south of London and, once the train had chuffed away from the platform, full of fresh air swaying the trees. Tonino breathed the air deeply and began to get his colour back.

"Bad traveller, is he?" Mordecai Roberts asked sympathetically as he led them to the cab waiting for them outside the station.

This Mr Mordecai Roberts always puzzled Cat slightly. With his light, almost white, curly hair and his dark coffee complexion, he looked a great deal more foreign than Tonino did, and yet when he spoke it was in perfect, unforeign English. It was educated English, too, which was another puzzle, because Cat had always vaguely supposed that Mr Roberts was a sort of valet hired to look after Gabriel de Witt in his retirement. But Mr Roberts also seemed to be a strong magic user. He looked at Cat rather reproachfully as they got into the cab and said, "There are hundreds of spells against travel sickness, you know."

"I think I did stop him being sick," Cat said uncomfortably. Here was his old problem again, of not being sure when he was using magic and when he was not. But what really made Cat uncomfortable was the knowledge that if he *had* used magic on Tonino, it was not for Tonino's sake. Cat hated seeing people be sick. Here he was doing a good thing for a bad selfish reason again. At this rate he was, quite definitely, going to end up as an evil enchanter.

Gabriel de Witt lived in a spacious, comfortable modern house with wide windows and a metal rail along the roof in the latest style. It was set among trees in a new road that gave the house a view of the countryside beyond.

Miss Rosalie threw open its clean white front door and welcomed them all inside. She was a funny little woman with a lot of grey in her black hair, who always, invariably, wore grey lace mittens. She was another puzzle. There was a big gold wedding-ring lurking under the grey lace of her left-hand mitten, which Cat *thought* might mean she was married to Mr Roberts, but she always had to be called Miss Rosalie. For another thing, she behaved as if she was a witch. But she wasn't. As she shut the front door, she made brisk gestures as if she were setting wards of safety on it. But it was Mr Roberts who really set the wards.

"You'll have to go upstairs, boys," Miss Rosalie said. "I kept him in bed today. He was fretting himself ill about meeting young Antonio. So excited about the new magic. Up this way."

They followed Miss Rosalie up the deeply carpeted stairs and into a big sunny bedroom, where white curtains were gently blowing at the big windows. Everything possible was white: the walls, the carpet, the bed with its stacked white pillows and white bedspread, the spray of lilies-of-the-valley on the bedside table – and so neat that it looked like a room no one was using.

"Ah, Eric Chant and Antonio Montana!" Gabriel de Witt said from the bank of pillows. His thin dry voice sounded quite eager. "Glad to see you. Come and take a seat where I can look at you."

Two plain white chairs had been set one on each side of the bed and about halfway down it. Tonino slid sideways into the nearest, looking thoroughly intimidated. Cat could understand that. He thought, as he went round to the other chair, that the whiteness of the room must be to make Gabriel de Witt show up. Gabriel was so thin and pale that you would hardly have seen him among ordinary colours. His white hair melted into the white of the pillows. His face had shrunk so that it seemed like two caves, made from Gabriel's jutting cheekbones and his tall white forehead, out of which two strong eyes glared feverishly. Cat tried not to look at the tangle of white chest hair sticking out of the white nightshirt under Gabriel's too-pointed chin. It seemed indecent, somehow.

But probably the most upsetting thing, Cat thought as he sat down, was the smell of illness and old man in the room, and the way that, in spite of the whiteness, there was a darkness at the edges of everything. The corners of the room felt grey, and they loomed. Cat kept his eyes on Gabriel's long, veiny, enchanter's hands, folded together on the white bedspread, because these seemed the most normal things about him, and hoped this visit would not last too long.

"Now, young Antonio," Gabriel said, and his pale lips moved in a dry way Cat could not look at, "I hear that your best magic is done when you use someone else's spell."

Tonino nodded timidly. "I think so, sir."

Cat kept his eyes on Gabriel's unmoving, folded hands and braced himself for an hour or more of talk about Magic

Theory. But, to his surprise, the kind of talk Cat could not understand only went on for about five minutes. Then Gabriel was saying, "In that case, I would like to try a little experiment, with your permission. A very little simple one. As you can see, I am very feeble today. I would like to do a small enchantment to enable myself to sit up, but I believe it would not come to much without your help. Would you do that for me?"

"Of course," Tonino said. "Would – would a strength-spell be correct for this? I would have to sing, if that is all right, because that is the way we do things in the Casa Montana."

"By all means," agreed Gabriel. "When you're ready then."

Tonino put back his head and sang, to Cat's surprise, very sweetly and tunefully, in what seemed to be Latin, while Gabriel's hands moved on the bedspread, just slightly. As the song finished, the pillows behind Gabriel's head rebuilt themselves into a swelling stack, which pushed the old man into sitting position. After that, they pushed him away from themselves so that he was sitting up on his own, quite steadily.

"Well done!" said Gabriel. He was clearly delighted. A faint pink crept over his jutting cheeks and his eyes glittered in their caves. "You have very strong and unusual magic, young man." He turned eagerly to Cat. "Now I can talk to you, Eric. This is important. Are your remaining lives quite safe? I have reason to believe that someone is looking for them as well as for mine."

Cat's mind went to a certain cardboard book of matches, more than half of them used. "Well, Chrestomanci has them locked in the castle safe, with a lot of spells on them. They feel all right."

Gabriel's eyes glittered into distance while he considered Cat's lives too. "True," he said. "They feel secure. But I was never totally happy while Christopher's other life was locked in there. I put his last life into a gold ring, you know, and locked it in that same safe – this was at a time when he seemed to be losing a life once a week, and something had to be done, you understand – but it was a great relief to me when he married and we could give the life to Millie as her wedding ring. I would greatly prefer it if your lives were equally well guarded. A book of matches is such a flimsy thing."

Cat knew this. But Chrestomanci seemed to him to be the best guardian there could be. "Who do you think is looking for them?" he asked.

"Now that is the odd thing," Gabriel answered, still looking into distance. "The only person who seems to fit the shapes of the magics I am sensing has, I swear, been dead and gone at least two hundred years. An enchanter known as Neville Spiderman. He was one of the last of the really bad ones."

Cat stared at Gabriel staring into distance like a bony old prophet. On the other side of the bed, Tonino was staring too, looking as scared as Cat felt. "What," Cat asked huskily, "makes you think it might be someone from the past?"

"For this reason—" Gabriel began.

Then the thing Cat had been dreading happened.

Gabriel de Witt's face suddenly lost all expression. Behind him, the pillows began slowly subsiding, letting the old man down into lying position again. As they did so, Gabriel de Witt seemed to climb out of himself. A tall old man in a long white nightshirt unfolded himself from the old man who was lying down and stood for a moment looking rather sadly from Cat to Tonino, before he walked away into a distance that was somehow not part of the white bedroom.

Both their heads turned to follow him as he walked. Cat realised he could see Tonino through the shape of the departing old man, and the lilies-of-the-valley on the bedside table, and then the corner of the white wardrobe. The old man was getting smaller all the time as he walked, until at last he was lost into white distance.

Cat was astonished not to find himself screaming – although he almost did when he looked back at Gabriel de Witt lying on his pillows and found Gabriel's face blue-pale and more sunken than ever, and his mouth slowly dropping wider and wider open. Cat could not seem to utter a sound, or move either, until Tonino whispered, "I saw you *through* him!"

Cat gulped. "Me too. I saw you. Why was that?"

"Was that his last life?" Tonino asked. "Is he truly dead now?"

"I don't know," said Cat. "I think we ought to call someone."

But it seemed as if someone already knew. Footsteps thumped on the carpet outside and Miss Rosalie burst into the room, followed by Mr Roberts, who both rushed to the bed and stared anxiously down at Gabriel de Witt as if they expected him to wake up any minute. Cat snatched another look at that gaping mouth and strange, blue-wax complexion, and thought that he had never seen anyone more obviously dead. He had seen his parents just before their funeral, but they had looked almost asleep and not like this at all.

"Don't worry, boys," Miss Rosalie said. "It's only another life gone. He's still got two more."

"No, you're forgetting the life he gave to Asheth," Mr Roberts reminded her.

"Oh, so I am," Miss Rosalie said. "Silly of me. But he's still got one left. Why don't you go downstairs, boys, until the new life takes over. It can sometimes be quite a while."

Cat and Tonino jumped thankfully out of their chairs. But as they did so, Gabriel stirred. His mouth shut with a snap and his face became the face of a person again – a person who looked pale and unwell, but full of strong feelings despite that.

"Rosalie," he said, weak and fretful, "warn Chrestomanci. Neville Spiderman is sniffing round this house. I felt him very clearly just now."

"Oh, nonsense, Gabriel!" Miss Rosalie said, brisk and bossy. "How *could* he be? You *know* Neville Spiderman – whatever his real name was – lived at the time of the first Chrestomanci. That was more than a hundred years before you were born!"

"I felt him, I tell you!" Gabriel insisted. "He was there when my last life was leaving."

"You can't possibly know that," Miss Rosalie insisted.

"I do know. I made a study of the man," Gabriel insisted in return. His voice was more and more weak and quavery. "When I was first made Chrestomanci, I *studied* him, because I needed to know what a really evil enchanter was like and he was the most ingenious of the lot. And this is very ingenious, Rosalie. He's trying to make himself stronger than any Chrestomanci ever was. Warn Christopher he's not safe. Warn Eric particularly."

"Yes, yes, yes," Miss Rosalie said, so obviously humouring him that Gabriel began rolling about in distress, spilling bedclothes on to the floor. "Of course I'll warn them," Miss Rosalie said, hauling blankets back. "Settle down, Gabriel, before you make yourself ill, and we'll do everything you want." She made meaning faces at Mr Roberts to take Cat and Tonino out of the room.

Mr Roberts nodded. He put a hand on each boy's shoulder and steered them out on to the landing. Behind them, as he gently shut the door, they heard Gabriel say, "Listen, Rosalie, my mind is *not* wandering! Spiderman has learnt to travel in time. He's dangerous. I mean what I say."

Gabriel de Witt sounded so weak and so upset that Mr Roberts said, looking extremely worried, "Look, I think you boys had better go home now. I don't think he'll be well enough to talk to you again today. I'll call you a cab and telephone the castle to say you'll be back on an earlier train."

There was nothing Cat wanted more by this time. Tonino, from the look of him, felt the same. The only thing Cat regretted was that they were going to miss lunch. Still, Miss Rosalie's idea of lunch was usually a tomato and some lettuce, and they did have Millie's five shillings. He followed Mr Roberts downstairs thinking of doughnuts and station pies.

Luckily there was a cab just clopping along the road as they reached the front gate. It was one of those old-fashioned horse-drawn hackneys, like a big upright box on wheels, with the driver sitting up on top of the box. It was shabby and the horse was scrawny, but Mr Roberts hailed it with strong relief and paid the driver for them as the boys climbed in. "You can

25

just catch the twelve thirty," he said. "Hurry it along, driver."

He shut the door and the cab set off. It was smelly and jolting and its wheels squeaked, but Cat felt it was worth it just to get away so soon. It was not far to the station. Cat sat back in the half dark inside the box and felt his mind go empty with relief. He did not want to think of Gabriel de Witt again for a very long time. He thought about station pies and corned beef sandwiches instead.

But half an hour of jolting, smelling and squeaking later, something began puzzling him. He turned to the other boy in the dimness beside him. "Where were we going?"

Tonino – if that was his name: Cat found he was not at all sure – shook his head uncertainly. "We are travelling north east," he said. "I feel sick."

"Keep swallowing then," Cat told him. One thing he seemed to be sure of was that he was supposed to look after this boy, whoever he was. "It can't be that far now," he said soothingly. Then he wondered what, or where, was 'not far'. He was a little puzzled to find he had no idea.

At least he seemed to be right about its not being far. Five minutes later, just as the other boy's swallowing was getting quite desperate, the cab squealed to a stop with a great yell of "Woa there!" from the driver up above, and the door beside Cat was pulled open. Cat blinked out into grey light upon a dirty pavement and a row of old, old houses as far as he could see in both directions. We must be in the outskirts of London, he thought. While Cat puzzled about this, the driver said, "Two blondie lads, just like you said, governor."

The person who had opened the door leaned round it to

26

peer in at them. They found themselves face to face with a smallish elderly man in a dirty black gown. The peering round brown eyes and the brown whiskery face, full of lines and wrinkles, were so like a monkey's that it was only the soft black priestly sort of hat on the man's head that showed he was a man and not a monkey. Or probably not. Cat found, in some strange way, that he was not sure of anything.

The monkey's flat mouth spread in a grin. "Ah yes, the right two," the man said, "as ordered." He had a dry, snapping voice, which snapped out, "Out you get then. Make haste now."

While Cat and Tonino obediently scrambled out to find themselves in a long street of the old tumbledown houses – all slightly different, like cottages built for a town – the man in the black gown handed up a gold coin to the driver. "Charmed to take you back," he muttered. It was hard to tell if he was speaking to himself or to the driver, but the driver touched his hat to him anyway with great respect, cracked his whip and drove away, squealing and clattering. The cab seemed to move away from them up the tumbledown street in jerks, and each jerk seemed to make it harder to see. Before it quite reached the end of the street, it had jerked out of sight entirely.

They stared after it. "Why did that happen?" Tonino asked.

"Belongs to the future, doesn't it?" the monkey-like man snapped. Again, he might have been talking to himself. But he seemed to notice them then. "Come along now. No stupid questions. It's not every day I hire two apprentices from the poorhouse and I want you indoors earning your keep. Come along."

He turned and hurried into the house beside them. They followed, quite bewildered, past an unpainted front door – which closed with a slam behind them – into a dark, wooden hallway. Beyond this was a big room which was much lighter because of a row of filthy windows looking out on to bushes. As the monkey-man hurried them on through it, Cat recognised the place as a magician's workshop. It breathed out the smell of magic and of dragon's blood, and there were symbols chalked over most of the floor. Cat had a tantalising feeling that he should have known what most of those symbols were supposed to do, and that they were not quite in any order he was used to, but when he thought about this, the symbols meant nothing to him.

The main thing he noticed was the row of star charts along one wall. There were eight of them, getting newer and newer from the old, brown one at the far left, to the one on the right, after a gap where a ninth chart had been torn down, which was white and freshly drawn.

"Gave up on that one. Too well protected," the monkey-man remarked as Cat looked at the gap. Again he was probably talking to himself, for he swung round at once and opened a door at the end of the room. "Come along, come along," he snapped and hurried on down a sideways flight of stone steps into the cold stone basement under the house. Cat, as he hurried after, only had time to think that the last chart, after the torn-down one, had looked uncomfortably familiar in some way, before the monkey-man swung round on both of them at the bottom of the steps. "Now then," he said, "what are your names?"

It seemed a perfectly reasonable thing to ask, but they stood shivering on the chilly flagstones, staring from him to one another. Neither of them had the least idea.

The man sighed at their stupidity. "Too much of the forgettery," he muttered in that way that seemed to be talking to himself. He pointed to Cat. "All right," he said to Tonino. "What's *his* name?"

"Er—" said Tonino, "it means something. In Latin, I think. Felix, or something like that. Yes, Felix."

"And," the man said to Cat, "*his* name is?"

"Tony," said Cat. This did not strike him as quite right, any more than Felix did, but he did not seem to be able to get any closer than that. "His name's Tony."

"Not Eric?" snapped the man. "Which of you is Eric?"

They both shook their heads, although Cat had a faint, fleeting idea that the name meant a protected kind of heather. That was such an idiotic idea that he gave it up at once.

"Very well," snapped the man. "Tony and Felix, you are now my apprentices. This room here is where you will eat and sleep. You will find mattresses over there." He pointed a brown hairy hand at a dim corner. "In that other corner, there are brooms and a dustpan. I require you to sweep this room and make it as clean and tidy as you can. When that is done, you may lay out the mattresses."

"Please, sir—" Tonino began. He stopped, looking frightened, as the withered old monkey face swung round to stare at him. Then he said something that was obviously not what he had started to say. "Please, sir, what should we call you?"

"I am known as Master Spiderman," snapped the man. "You will address me as Master."

Cat felt a small, chilly jolt of alarm at the name. He put it down to the fact that he was already disliking this monkey-faced old man very much indeed. There was a smell that came off him, of old clothes, mustiness and illness, which reminded Cat of – of – of something he could not quite remember, except that it made him frightened and uneasy. So, to make himself feel better, he said what he knew Tonino had really been going to say.

"Sir, we haven't had any lunch yet."

Master Spiderman's round monkey eyes blinked Cat's way. "Is that so? Well, you may have food as soon as you have swept and tidied this room." At that, he turned and ran up the stone steps to the door, with his musty black coat swirling. He stopped at the top. "Do not try to do any magic," he said. "I'll have nothing like that here. Nothing stupid. This place is in a time apart from any other time and you must behave yourselves here." He went out through the door and shut it behind him. They heard a bolt shoot home on the other side of it.

That door was the only way out of the basement. The only other opening in the stone walls was a high up window, fast shut and too dirty to see through, which let in a meagre grey light. Cat and Tonino stared from the door to the window, and then at one another. "What did he mean," asked Tonino, "to do no magic? Can you do magic?"

"I don't *think* so," said Cat. "Can you?"

"I – I can't remember," Tonino said miserably. "I am blank."

So was Cat, whenever he thought about it. He was uncertain of everything, including why they were here and whether he ought to be frightened about it, or just miserable. He clung to the two things he was certain about. Tonino was younger than he was and Cat ought to be looking after him.

Tonino was shivering. "Let's find the brooms and start sweeping," Cat said. "It'll warm us up and he'll give us something to eat when we've done it."

"He *might*," Tonino said. "Do you believe him or trust him?"

"No," said Cat. This was something else his fuzzy mind was clear about completely. "We'd better not give him an excuse not to give us any food."

They found two worn down brooms and a long-handled dustpan in the corner by the stairs, along with a heap of amazingly various rubbish – rusty cans, cobwebby planks, rags so old they had turned into piles of dirt, walking sticks, broken jars, butterfly nets, fishing rods, half a carriage wheel, broken umbrellas, works of clocks and things that had decayed too much for anyone to guess what they had once been – and they set about cleaning the room.

Without needing to discuss it, they started at the end where the stairs were. It was clearer that end. The rest of the room was filled with a clutter of old splintery work benches and broken chairs, which got more and more jumbled towards the far end, where the entire wall was completely draped in cobwebs, thicker and dustier than Cat would have thought possible. For another thing, when they were near the stairs, they could hear Master Spiderman creaking and muttering about in the room overhead and it seemed reasonable to think that he could hear them too. It was in both their minds that, if he heard them truly hard at work, he might decide to bring them something to eat.

They swept for what seemed hours. They used the least smelly of the old rags for dusters. Cat found an old sack, into which they noisily poured panloads of dust, cobwebs and broken glass. They thumped with their brooms. Tonino hauled out another load of rubbish from another corner, making a tremendous clatter, and found the mattresses among it. They were filthy, lumpy things, so damp they felt wet.

Cat slammed about making a heap of the most broken chairs and hung the mattresses over it in a gust of mildew-smell, to air. By this time, slightly to Cat's surprise, more than half the room was clear. Dust hung in the air, making Tonino's nose and eyes run, filling their clothes and their hair, and streaking their faces with grey. Their hands were black and their fingernails blacker. They were hungry, thirsty, and tired out.

"I need a drink," Tonino croaked.

Cat swept the stairs a second time, very noisily, but Master Spiderman gave no sign of having heard. Perhaps if he called out…? It seemed to take a real effort to muster the courage. And, somehow, Cat could not bring himself to call Master Spiderman "Master", try as he would. He knocked politely on the door and called out, "Excuse me, sir! Excuse me, please, we're terribly thirsty."

There was no reply. When Cat put his ear to the door he could no longer hear any sounds of Master Spiderman moving about. He came gloomily back down the stairs. "I don't think he's there now."

Tonino sighed. "He will know when this room is cleared and he will come back then, but not before. I am fairly sure he is an enchanter."

"There's nothing to stop us having a rest anyway," Cat said. He dragged the two mattresses over to the wall and made a seat out of them. They both sat down thankfully. The mattresses were still extremely damp and they smelt horrible. Both of them tried not to notice. "How do you know he's an enchanter?" Cat asked, to take his mind off the smell and the wetness.

"The eyes," said Tonino. "Your eyes are the same."

Cat thought of Master Spiderman's round, glossy eyes and shuddered. "They're nothing *like* the same!" he said. "My eyes are blue."

Tonino put his head down and held it in both hands. "Sorry," he said. "For a moment I thought you were an enchanter. Now I don't know what I think."

This made Cat shift about uncomfortably. It was frightening, if he let himself notice it, how whenever he thought about anything, particularly about magic, there seemed to be nothing to think. There seemed to be only here and now in this cold basement, and the horrible bad-breath smell coming up from the mattresses, and the damp creeping up with the smell and coming through his clothes.

Beside him, Tonino was shivering again. "This is no good," Cat said. "Get up."

Tonino climbed to his feet. "I think it is a spell to keep us obedient," he said. "He told us we could lay the mattresses out *after* the room was clean."

"I don't care," said Cat. He picked up the top mattress and shook it, trying to shake the smell – or the spell – out.

This proved to be a bad mistake. The whole basement became full, almost instantly, of thick, choking, bad-smelling, chaffy dust. They could hardly see one another. What Cat could see of Tonino was alarming. He was bending over coughing and coughing, a terrible hacking cough, with a whooping, choking sound whenever Tonino tried to breathe in. It sounded as if Tonino was choking to death, and it frightened Cat out of what few wits he seemed to have.

He dropped the mattress in a further cloud of dust, snatched up a broom and ran up the stairs in a frenzy of fear and guilt, where he battered on the door with the broom handle. "Help!" he screamed. "Tony's suffocating! *Help!*"

Nothing happened. As soon as Cat stopped beating on the door, he could tell from the sort of silence beyond that Master Spiderman was not bothering to listen. He ran down again, into the thick, thick dust, seized the choking Tonino by one elbow and pushed him up the stairs.

"Get up by the door," he said. "It's clearer there." He could hear Tonino choking his way upwards as he himself ran towards the dirty, murky high-up window and slammed the end of the broom handle into it like a spear.

Cat had meant to smash out a pane. But the grimy glass simply splintered into a white star and would not break any further however hard Cat poked at it with the broom. By this time he was coughing almost as wretchedly as Tonino. And angry. Master Spiderman was trying to break their spirits. Well, he was not going to! Cat dragged one of the heavy, splintery work benches under the window and climbed on it.

The window was one of the kind that slides up and down. Standing on the bench brought Cat's nose level with the rusty old catch that held the two halves shut in the middle. He took hold of the catch and wrenched at it angrily. It came to pieces in his hand, but at least it was not holding the window shut any more. Cat threw the broken pieces down and gripped the dirty frame with both sets of fingers. And pulled. And heaved. And rattled.

"Let me help," Tonino said hoarsely, climbing up beside Cat, and breathed out hugely because he had been holding his breath as he came across the room.

Cat moved to one side gratefully and they both pulled. To their joy, the top half of the window juddered and slid, making an opening about four inches wide above their heads. Through it, they could just see the bottom of a set of railings, level with the pavement outside, and pairs of feet walking past – feet in old-fashioned sort of shoes with high heels and buckles on the front.

This struck them as strange. So did the way that warm wafts of fresh air came blowing in their faces through the open gap at the same time as clouds of the dust went streaming out. But they did not stop to think about either of these things. It had dawned on both of them that if they could pull the top half of the window right down, they could climb through and get away. They hung by their hands from the top of the window, pulling grimly.

But no amount of pulling seemed to get the window any further open. As Cat left off, panting, Tonino hammered the lower half of the window with his fist and shouted at the next pair of buckled shoes that walked past.

"Help! Help! We're shut in!"

The feet went by without pausing.

"They didn't hear," said Cat. "It must be a spell."

"Then what do we *do*?" Tonino wailed. "I am so hungry!"

So was Cat. As far as he could tell, it was at least teatime by then. He thought of tea going on at the castle, with cress sandwiches and cream cakes – Hang on! What castle? But the flash of memory was gone, leaving just the notion of cress sandwiches, luxurious ones with all the crusts cut off, and cakes oozing jam and cream. Cat's stomach grumbled and he felt ready to wail like Tonino. But he knew he had to be sensible, because he was older than Tonino.

"He said we could have food when we'd cleaned the whole room," he reminded Tonino. "We'd better get on and finish it."

They climbed down and set to work again. This time, Cat tried to organise it properly. He made sure they worked only in short bursts and he found two not-so-broken chairs so that they could sit on them and rest while the latest lot of dust was sucked away out through open window. Slowly they worked their way towards the far end of the basement. By the time the light filtering in past the dirt on the window was golden, late evening light, they were ready to start on the end wall.

They were not looking forward to this. From ceiling to floor, that end was draped in a mass of filthy, dust-hung cobwebs at least two feet thick, fluttering and heaving, grey and sinister in the small draught from the window. Under the draped webs, they could just see another of the splintery work benches. On it, in the very middle, there seemed to be a small black container of some kind.

"What do you think that is?" Tonino wondered.

"I'll see. More old rubbish, I expect." Cat shudderingly put his left hand through the cobwebs, hating the sticky, tender touch of them, and took hold of the black thing.

As soon as his fingers closed round it, he had a feeling it was important. But when he had pulled it gently out, avoiding touching the cobwebs where he could, it was just an old black cannister with a round hole clumsily punched in its lid. "Only a tin tea caddy," he said. "It looks as if someone's tried to make it into a money box." He shook it. Something inside rattled quite sharply.

"See what's in there," said Tonino. "It might be valuable."

Cat pried at the lid, getting a big new patch of black dirt on his front as he did so. The tin was coated in generations of sooty grease. But the lid was quite easy to move and came off with a clatter. Inside were a very few red kidney beans. Seven of them.

Cat tipped them out on to his hand to be sure, and they were indeed, most disappointingly, beans. They must have been in that tin a very long time. Four of them were wrinkled and shrivelled, and one was so old it was just a withered brown lump. It was clear they were nothing valuable at all.

"Beans!" Cat said disgustedly.

"Oh yes," said Tonino, "but think of Jack and the Beanstalk."

They stared at one another. In an enchanter's basement anything was possible. Both had visions of mighty bean plants growing through the ceiling and on through the roof of the house, and each of them climbing one, away from Master Spiderman and out of his power. And while they stared, they heard the sound of the door being unbolted at the other end of the room.

Cat hastily thrust the handful of beans into his pocket and jammed the lid back on the cannister while Tonino picked up his broom. Tonino waited until Cat had carefully put the old tin back through the cobwebs, into the dust-free circle on the wooden bench where it had stood before, and then reached up with the broom and began virtuously sweeping billows of cobweb off the wall.

Master Spiderman threw open the door and raced down the stone steps, shouting, "No, no, no, you wretched boy! Stop that at once! Don't you know a spell when you see one?" He came rushing through the room and advanced on Tonino with his hand raised in a fist.

Tonino dropped the broom with a clatter and backed away. Cat was not sure whether Master Spiderman was going to hit Tonino or cast a spell on him, but he got between them quickly anyway. "You've no call to hurt him," he said. "You told us to clean the place up."

For a moment, Master Spiderman bent over the two of them, clearly seething with rage. Cat smelt the unclean old-man smell from Master Spiderman's breath and the mildew from his black coat. He looked into the round glaring eyes, and at the moving wrinkles and long hairs on Master Spiderman's face, and he felt as much sick as he was frightened.

"*And* you promised us some food when we'd done it," he added.

Master Spiderman ignored this, but he seemed to control his rage a little. "For this spell," he said, in that way he had of almost talking to himself. There were little flecks of white round his wide, lipless mouth. "For this spell, I have kept myself alive for countless years beyond my natural span. This spell will change the world. This spell will give me the world! And one miserable boy nearly ruins it by trying to sweep it off the wall!"

"I didn't know it was a spell," Tonino protested. "What is it supposed to do?"

Master Spiderman laughed – a private sort of laugh, with his mouth closed as if he were shutting in secrets. "Supposed?" he said. "It is *supposed* to make a *ten*-lifed enchanter, who is to be more powerful than any of your Chrestomancis. It *will* do so, as long as neither of you meddles with it again. Don't dare *touch* it!"

He stepped around them and made gestures at the wall, rather as if he were plaiting or twisting something. The grey swathe of cobweb which Tonino had brought down billowed itself and lifted upwards. Master Spiderman made flattening and twiddling motions with his hands then, and the cobwebs began moving this way and that, growing thicker as they moved, and wafting themselves up to stick to the ceiling. Cat thought he could see a host of little half-invisible creeping things scurrying about among the grey swathes, repairing the spell the way Master Spiderman wanted it, and had to look away. Tonino, however, stared at them, amazed and interested.

"There," Master Spiderman said at last. "Don't go near it again." He turned to leave.

"Hang on," said Cat. "You promised us something to eat. Sir," he added quickly, as Master Spiderman swung angrily round at him. "We have cleaned the room, sir."

"I'll give you food," Master Spiderman said, "when you tell me which of you is Eric."

As before, the name meant nothing to either of them. But they were both so hungry by then that Cat instantly pointed to Tonino and Tonino just as promptly pointed at Cat. "He is," they said in chorus.

"I see," snapped Master Spiderman. "You don't know." He swung round again and hurried away, muttering to himself. The mutters turned into distinct speech while Master Spiderman was clambering up the steps. He must have thought they could not hear him from there. "I don't know which of you is either, damn it! I'll just have to kill both of you – one of you more than once, I imagine."

As the door shut with a boom, Cat and Tonino stared at one another, really frightened for the first time. "Let's try the window again," Cat said.

But the window still would not budge. Cat was standing on the work bench wagging the broom handle out through the open space in hopes of breaking the spell on it, when he heard the door opening again. He came down hastily and kept hold of the broom for a weapon.

Master Spiderman came through the door with a lighted lamp, which he put down on the top step. They were glad to see the light. It was getting quite dark in the basement by then.

They watched Master Spiderman turn and push a tray out on to the top step beside the lamp. "Here is your supper, boys," he said. "And here is what I want you to do next. Listen carefully. I want you to watch that spell at the end of the room. Don't take your eyes off it. And the moment you see anything different about it, you are to come and knock on the door and tell me. Do that, and you shall have a currant cake each as a reward."

There was a sort of oily friendliness about Master Spiderman now which made both boys very uneasy. Cat nudged Tonino and Tonino at once began trying to find out what this new friendliness was about. "What are you expecting to happen to the spell?" he asked, looking very earnest and innocent.

"So we know what to look for," Cat explained.

Master Spiderman hesitated, obviously wondering what to tell them. "You will see a disturbance," he said. "Yes, a disturbance among the webs. It will look quite strange, but you must not be frightened. It will only be the soul of an enchanter who is presently on his deathbed, and it will, almost at once, turn harmlessly into a bean. Make sure that the bean has dropped correctly into the container on the bench and then tell me. Then you shall each have a currant cake. You will do that and you shall have a cake each. You are good boys, are you not?"

"Oh yes," they both assured him.

"Good." Master Spiderman backed out through the door and shut it again.

Cat and Tonino went cautiously up the stairs to look at the tray. On it was a tin jug of water, a small stale loaf, and a block of cheese so old and sweaty that it looked like a piece of soap someone had just washed with.

"Do you think it's poisoned?" Tonino whispered.

Cat thought about it. In a way, it was a triumph, that they had forced Master Spiderman to give them anything to eat, but it was quite plain that, even so, Master Spiderman was not going to waste decent food on people he was planning to kill. Giving them this food was just to lull them. "No," Cat said. "He'd use better food. I bet it's the currant cakes that are going to be poisoned."

Tonino was evidently thinking as well, while they carried the lamp and the tray down the steps and set both up on a work bench in the middle of the room. "He said," he observed, "that he has kept himself alive much longer than his normal lifetime. Do you think he does this by killing boys – his apprentices?"

Cat dragged the two least rickety chairs up beside the bench. "I don't know," he said, "but he might. I think when that enchanter's ghost gets here, we ought to ask it to help."

"A good idea," said Tonino. Then he added dubiously, "If it *can*."

"Of course it can," Cat said. "He'll still be an enchanter even if he *is* a ghost."

They tore the hard bread into lumps and set to work to gnaw at these and the rubbery cheese, taking it in turns to swig water out of the tin jug. The water tasted stale and pond-like. Cat's stomach began to hurt almost at once. Perhaps, he thought, his reasoning had been wrong and this nasty supper was poisoned after all. On the other hand, it could be that this food was simply indigestible – or just that the mere idea of poison had made his stomach think it *was*.

He watched Tonino carefully to see if he was showing any signs of poisoning. But Tonino evidently trusted Cat's judgement. Under the soft lamplight, Tonino's eyes became brighter as he ate and his dirty drawn-looking cheeks became rounder and pinker. Cat watched him use his teeth to scrape the very last of the cheese off the rind and decided that there was no poison in this food. His stomach unclenched a little.

"I'm still hungry," Tonino said, laying the rind down regretfully. "I'm so hungry I could even eat those dry beans."

Cat remembered that he had crammed those beans into his pocket when Master Spiderman had come charging down the steps. He fetched them out and laid all seven under the lamp. He was surprised to see that they were glossier and plumper than they had been. Four of them had lost their wrinkles entirely. Even the oldest and most withered one looked more like a bean and less like a dried brown lump. They glowed soft reds and purples under the light. "I wonder," he said, pushing at them with a finger. "I wonder if these are all enchanters too."

"They might be," Tonino said, staring at them. "He said he was to make a ten-lifed enchanter. Here might be seven lives, with an eighth one coming soon. Where does he get the other two lives from though?"

From us, Cat thought, and hoped that Tonino would not think of this too.

But at that moment, the newest and glossiest bean gave a sudden jump and flipped over, end to end. Tonino forgot what they had been talking about and leaned over it, fascinated.

"This one is alive! Are all the others living too?"

It seemed that they were. One by one, each of the beans stirred and then flipped, until they were all rolling and hopping about, even the oldest bean, although this one only seemed to be able to rock from side to side. The newest bean was now flipping so vigorously that it nearly jumped off the work bench. Cat caught it and put it back among the others. "I wonder if they're going to grow," he said.

"Beanstalks," Tonino said. "Oh, please, yes!"

As he spoke, the newest bean split down its length to show a pale, greenish interior, which was clearly very much alive. But it was not so much like a bean growing. It was more like a beetle spreading its wings. For an instant, the boys could see the two mottled purplish-red halves of its skin, spread out like wing-covers, and then these seemed to melt into the rest of it. What spread out then was a pale, greenish, transparent growing thing. The growing thing very quickly spread into a flatness with several points, until it looked like nothing so much as a large floating sycamore leaf made of greenish light. There were delicate veins in it and it pulsed slightly.

By this time, five of the others were splitting and spreading too. Each grew points and veins, but in slightly different shapes, so that Cat thought of them as an ivy leaf, a fig leaf, a vine leaf, a maple leaf, and a leaf from a plane tree. Even the oldest, seventh bean was trying to split. But it was so withered and hard and evidently having such difficulty that Tonino put a forefinger on each half of it and helped it break open. "Oh, enchanters, please help us!" he said, as the bean spread into a smaller, more stunted shape.

Wild service tree leaf, Cat thought, and wondered a little how he knew about trees. He looked sadly at the cluster of frail, quivering, greenish shapes gathered by the base of the lamp and realised that Tonino had been right to be doubtful in the first place. The green shapes might once have been enchanters – Cat thought Tonino was right about that – but they were not ghosts. These beings were soft, helpless and bewildered. It was like asking newly hatched butterflies for help.

"I don't think they *can* help," he said. "They don't even know what's happened to them."

Tonino sighed. "They do feel awfully old," he agreed. "But they feel new too. We shall have to help them instead. Make them hide from Master Spiderman."

He tried to catch the old, stunted leaf, but it fluttered away from his fingers, frantically. This seemed to alarm the rest. They all fluttered and trembled and moved in a glowing group to safety behind the tin jug.

"Leave off! You're frightening them!" Cat said. As he said it, he heard a sort of scuffling from behind him, at the end of the room. He and Tonino both whipped round to look.

There, glowing faintly among the draped cobwebs, another leaf-shaped thing, a big one, was struggling among the clinging, dusty threads. It was struggling even more frantically than the stunted leaf had struggled to get away from Tonino, but every flap and wriggle only brought it further into the midst of the tangled webs and lower and lower towards the black cannister.

"This is the dead enchanter!" Tonino said. "Oh, quickly! Help it!"

Cat got up slowly. He was rather afraid of the thing. It was like the times when a bird gets into your bedroom – a panic that was desperately catching – but when he saw the thing suddenly turn into a bean and plummet towards the black cannister he raced to the end of the room and pushed his hands nervously into the grey tangled shrouds of cobweb. He was just in time to deflect it with the edge of his left hand. The bean pinged against the cannister and bounced out on to the floor. Cat scooped it up. The instant it was in his hand, the bean split and grew and became a bigger, brighter and more pointed leaf-shape than any of the others. Cat carried it, whirring between his hands, and deposited it carefully beside the rest, where it lay beside the others as part of a transparent, pulsing, living group, shining under the lamp. Like a shoal of fish, Cat thought.

"He's coming!" gasped Tonino. "Make them escape!"

Cat heard the door at the top of the steps opening. He flapped his hands at the cluster of leaf-shapes. "Shoo!" he whispered. "Hide somewhere!" All the leaf-shapes flinched from his hands but, maddeningly, they all stayed where they were, hovering behind the tin jug.

"Oh, *go!*" Tonino implored them as Master Spiderman came storming down the steps. But they would not move.

"What are you boys playing at?" Master Spiderman demanded. He went hurrying through the room towards the draped cobwebs. "According to my star chart, Gabriel de Witt died nearly twenty minutes ago. His soul must have arrived here by now. Why have you not knocked on the door? Are you too busy feeding your faces to notice? Is that it?"

He stormed past the lamp and the work bench without looking at them. All the leaf-shapes flinched as the angry gust of his passing hit them. Then, to Cat's extreme relief, the big new leaf-shape lifted one side of itself in a sort of beckoning gesture and slid quietly over the edge of the bench into the shadows underneath it. The others turned themselves and flitted after it, like a row of flatfish diving, with the old, stunted one hastening after in last place. Cat and Tonino turned their eyes sideways to make sure they were hidden and then looked quickly back at Master Spiderman. He was hurling cobwebs right and left in order to get at the black cannister.

He snatched it up. He shook it. He turned round clutching it to his chest, in such amazement and despair that Cat almost felt sorry for him. "It's empty!" he said. His face was the face of the saddest monkey in the most unkind zoo in any world. "Empty!" he repeated. "All gone – all the souls I have collected are gone! The souls of seven nine-lifed enchanters are missing and the new one is not here! My lifetime's work! What has gone wrong?" As he asked this, the grief in his face hardened suddenly to anger and suspicion. "What have you boys done?"

Cat had been prepared to feel very frightened when Master Spiderman realised it was their fault. He was slightly surprised to feel more tense than frightened, and quite businesslike. It was a great help to have Tonino opposite him, looking calm and sturdy. "They got out," he said.

"They started to grow," Tonino said. "They were beans, you know, and beans grow. Why are you upset, sir? Were you meaning to swallow them?"

"Of *course* I was!" Master Spiderman more or less howled. "I have been intercepting the souls of dead Chrestomancis for more than two hundred *years*, you stupid little boy! When there were nine, and I swallowed them, I would be the strongest enchanter there has ever been! And you let them get out!"

"But there were only eight," Tonino pointed out.

Master Spiderman hugged the cannister to himself and spread his mouth into a wide smile. "No," he said. "Nine. One of you boys has my ninth soul – and the other eight have no way to get out of this room." And he shouted, loudly and suddenly, "*Where have they gone?*"

Cat and Tonino both jumped and tried to look as if they had no idea. But the shout obviously terrified the dead souls lurking under the table. One of the middle-sized ones, the one like a fig leaf, made a dash for freedom, between the broken rungs of Cat's chair and out towards the stairs and the open door at the top. The others all followed an instant later, as if they could not bear to be left behind, streaming after it in a luminous line.

"Aha!" shouted Master Spiderman. He dropped the cannister and ran at an incredible speed through the room and up the first three stairs, where he was just in time to block the path of the escaping souls. Above him, the door banged shut. The line of leaf shapes swirled to a stop almost level with the lowest stair, where they dithered in the air a little and then darted away sideways with the big new soul in the lead and the smallest, oldest one fluttering rather desperately in the rear.

At this, Master Spiderman leapt down the steps and snatched up a butterfly net from the heap of rubbish. "Lively, are you?" he muttered. "Soon put a stop to that!" Two more butterfly nets left the heap and planted themselves, one in Cat's hand and one in Tonino's. "You let them out," he said. "You get them caught again." And with that, he went leaping after the streaming line of souls with his butterfly net held sideways to scoop them up.

Cat and Tonino jumped up and began pretending to chase the fleeing souls too, getting in Master Spiderman's way whenever they could. Tonino galumphed backwards and forwards, waving his net and shouting, "Got you!" and "Oh bother, I *missed*!" in all the wrong places, and particularly when he was nowhere near the streaming line of souls. Cat sprinted beside Master Spiderman and, whenever Master Spiderman lunged to scoop up the souls, Cat made sure to lunge too, and either to jog Master Spiderman's elbow or to cross Master Spiderman's butterfly net with his own so that he missed.

Master Spiderman howled and snarled at him, but he was too intent on catching the souls to do anything to Cat. Round the basement they sped, like people in a mad game of lacrosse, with Tonino galloping in the middle, upsetting broken furniture into their path, while the line of shining, desperately frightened souls sped round the room at waist level, swerved outwards to miss the draped cobwebs, and rushed along the wall with the window in it, slightly higher up.

Window! Cat thought at them as he chased beside Master Spiderman. *Window's open!* But they were too frightened to notice the window and streamed on towards the steps again.

There, the ivy-leaf soul must have had the idea that the door was still open and tried to dart up the steps. The others all stopped and swirled round to follow it.

Seeing this, Master Spiderman shouted "Aha!" again and rushed towards them with his net ready. Cat and Tonino had to do some fast and artistic jumping about on the stairs, or the whole lot would have been scooped up there and then.

Then separate, you fools! Cat thought. *Why don't you all fly different ways?*

But this, it seemed, the terrified souls could not bear to do. Cat could feel them thinking that they would be lost if they were alone. They streamed on in a cluster, up into the corner of the room and then on round it again, just below the ceiling, with Master Spiderman close behind, net raised, and Cat pelting after him. There was a heart-stopping moment then when the old, small soul flew too near the draped cobwebs and got tangled in them. Again the other souls swirled to a stop and waited. Cat only got there just in time. Butterfly nets clashed as Cat managed to stumble into the cobwebs and carve them apart to let the trapped soul loose.

As it went fluttering after the others, Tonino galloped across the room and squeezed behind the bench that Cat had stood on to open the window. The bench went over with a crash. The line of souls had just gathered speed again, but this brought them almost to a standstill. Tonino stood waving his net back and forth beside the window, trying to give them a hint.

The souls understood – or at least the big new one which had been Gabriel de Witt seemed to. It made for the window in a glad swoop. The luminous green line of the others followed and all went whirling out through the gap into the dark night as if they had been sucked out by the draught.

Thank goodness! Cat thought, leaning on his butterfly net and panting. Now he won't need to kill us either.

Master Spiderman uttered a great scream of rage. "You opened the window! You broke my spells!" He made a throwing motion towards Cat and then at Tonino. Cat felt a light, strong stickiness close about him. He had barely time to think that it felt remarkably like when you brush through a cobweb by accident, before Master Spiderman was rushing up the basement steps. Cat and Tonino, sweaty and breathless and covered with dirt as they were, found they were forced to rush up the steps behind him.

"I am not letting you out of my sight from now on!" Master Spiderman panted as they pelted through the room overhead. They were going too fast for Tonino, who nearly fell on his face as they reached the hallway. Cat dragged him upright while Master Spiderman was hurling open the front door, and they pelted on, out into the street. It was pitch dark out there. Curtains were drawn over the windows of all the houses and there were no kind of streetlights anywhere. Master Spiderman stopped, panting heavily, and seemed to be staring wildly around.

For a second or so, Cat had hopes that the escaped souls had got away, or at least had had the sense to hide.

But the souls had no sense. They did not have proper brains to have sense *with*, Cat thought sadly. They were hovering in a little cluster at the end of the street, just as greenly luminous and easy to see as they had been in the basement, and bobbing anxiously together as if they were discussing what to do now.

"There!" Master Spiderman cried out triumphantly. He dived down the street, nearly pulling Cat and Tonino over.

"Oh fly away! Go somewhere safe!" Tonino panted as they stumbled on down the pavement.

The souls saw them at the last possible moment – or they made up their non-minds what to do, Cat was not sure which. At all events, as Master Spiderman's butterfly net was sweeping towards them, they swirled upwards in a spiral, with the big soul that had been Gabriel de Witt's leading, and vanished across the roof of the house on the corner.

Master Spiderman screamed with frustration and rose into the air too. Cat and Tonino were lugged up into the air after him, spinning and dangling sideways. Before they could right themselves, they were being towed across chimney pots and roofs at a furious speed.

By the time Cat had hauled on Tonino and Tonino had clutched at Cat, and they had discovered that they could use the butterfly nets they still held to balance themselves upright in the air, they were going even faster, with the wind of speed in their eyes and whipping at their hair. They could see the small green cluster of souls fleeing ahead of them above a ragged field with donkeys in it, and then above a wood. There was a big half moon that Cat had not noticed before, lying on its back among clouds, which served to show the souls up even more bright and green.

"Faster!" Master Spiderman snapped, as they all hurtled across the wood too.

"Go as fast as he does, go as fast as he does," Cat heard Tonino whisper.

This was exactly what seemed to happen. Master Spiderman snapped, "Faster!" several times, once when the moon vanished and there were suddenly a thousand more roofs and chimneys whirling beneath them; again when it came on to rain briefly; and yet again when there was a full moon shining down on some kind of park below. Yet the small green cluster of souls speeding ahead stayed precisely the same distance in front of them. The dark landscape underneath changed again, but they were still no nearer, and no further away either.

"Curses!" panted Master Spiderman. "They're travelling into the future. This is a hundred and fifty years now. Boys, give me your strength. I command it!"

Cat felt energy draining strongly out of him through the invisible cobwebs that were towing him after Master Spiderman. Although this was not a pleasant feeling, it seemed to lift some of the fuzzy blankness in his mind. Cat found dim memories flitting through his head as they sped on, of faces and places mostly – a castle, a handsome dark-haired man saying something sarcastic, a lady in mittens, a very old man lying in bed. And a smell. Around the very old man in bed there had hung the same musty, sick smell that came strongly, in gusts, off Master Spiderman as he whirled along in front. But Cat could not put these memories together to make sense. It was easier to notice that the chimney pots beneath now seemed to be growing out into the countryside, in lines along the sides of fields, and to listen to Tonino, who was still whispering, "Go as fast as we do, go as fast as we do!" over and over.

"Are you using his spell or something?" Cat whispered.

"I think so," Tonino whispered back. "I seem to remember doing this before."

Cat seemed to remember Tonino could do this sort of thing too, but before he could discover how he knew, the landscape below jerked into another different shape. There were handsome gas streetlights down there now, trees lining wide roads and houses that stood apart from one another in gardens. Ahead, the small glowing group of souls hurtled across a village green and then over a dimly gleaming railway line.

"I *know* this place!" Cat said. "I think we were here this morning."

Almost at the same time, Master Spiderman was making confused noises. "I thought he was taking them to his home," he said, "but we have passed it. Where are they *going* then?"

In front of them, the souls streamed above some tall trees and almost instantly dived down beyond, towards a tall building with rows of lighted windows. Still making puzzled noises, and grunting with the effort, Master Spiderman dragged himself and Cat and Tonino across the treetops after them.

They were in time to see the souls, in a luminous line with the big one still leading, go streaming sedately in through the big arched door in the middle of the building. At the sight, Master Spiderman yelled with rage and plunged them all downwards so quickly that Cat had to shut his eyes. It was even quicker than falling.

They landed with a fairly violent bump on what was luckily a soft lawn. Tonino and Cat got up quickly, but Master Spiderman was winded and staggered about gasping, looking so thin and bent and hollow-faced that he might almost have been a real monkey. They could see him clearly, propping himself on his butterfly net and puffing, because there was a large light over the arched door of the building. The light shone on letters carved into the stone of the arch: HOSPITAL OF THE SACRED HEART.

"A *hospital*!" Master Spiderman panted. "Why would they want to come *here*? Don't stand there staring, you stupid boys! We have to catch them!" And he was off again, using the butterfly net like a walking stick and muttering, "Oh *why* do I always get so *old* when I come to the future? Come on, you wretched boys, come *on*!"

He dragged them in through the doorway into a most obvious hospital corridor, long, pale green and well lit, and smelling so strongly of antiseptic that it drowned even the smell of Master Spiderman. Cat and Tonino both became extremely conscious of how dirty they were. They tried to hang back. But there near the end of the corridor, almost transparent yellow in the strong light, was the little cluster of souls, floating nervously near a staircase, as if they were again undecided what to do. The sight seemed to inspire Master Spiderman to a second wind. He broke into a gallop, waving his butterfly net, and the boys were dragged into a gallop too.

When they were halfway along the corridor, a nun came out of a doorway, carrying a kidney dish. She was one of those nuns with a headdress that was made of big starched points, like a ship in full sail.

Not a headdress to dodge in, Cat would have thought. But dodge she did as Master Spiderman came charging down on her like a wild monkey in a flying black coat, with Cat and Tonino helplessly sprinting behind him. The nun's headdress gave an outraged rattle, and she backed into a doorway, clutching her kidney dish and staring as they all rushed past.

The souls saw them coming and made up their minds. The big one darted for the staircase and the others went streaming after, up alongside the crisp green line painted on the wall. Master Spiderman hopped on one foot in order to stop, spun round and went hammering up the stairs behind them. So, perforce, did Cat and Tonino.

As they all got to the top, another nun was just coming through a swing door, holding it open with her back so that she could wrestle a big tray with bottles on it through the door too. The souls swirled neatly around her huge starched headdress and on into the ward beyond. The nun did not see them. But she saw Master Spiderman with his face stretched into a grin of effort bounding towards the door like a maniac monkey, and the two dirty, perspiring, cobwebby boys behind him. She dropped the tray and screamed.

Master Spiderman barged her aside and dashed into the ward, dragging the boys with him.

They were in a long, dimly lighted space with a row of beds on either side. The souls were about halfway down the room, flitting cautiously in their usual cluster. But the place was not quiet. Cat had the strange feeling that they had just burst into a rookery. The air rang with peculiar cawing noises.

It took him a second or so to realise that the cawing was coming from little white cradles that were hooked to the bottom of each bed. All the people in the beds were ladies, all looking rather exhausted, and in each cradle there was a tiny, wrinkly, red-faced new born baby – at least, there were two of them in the cradle nearest Cat – and it was the babies who were making the noise, more and more of them, as the nun's scream and the crash of the bottles, followed by the thunder of the door and the shout of anger Master Spiderman gave as he towed Cat and Tonino between the beds, woke every single baby there up.

"We're in a maternity ward," Cat said, wishing he could back straight out of here again.

Tonino was horribly out of breath, but he managed to grin. "I know. The souls are being clever after all."

Master Spiderman was shouting, "Stop them! Don't let them get into any babies! They'll be gone for good then!" He dived at the cluster of souls with his butterfly net raised.

The souls did seem to be showing intelligence at last. As Master Spiderman dived, they rose up in a group above his waving net and then peeled apart in eight different directions. For a second or so, Master Spiderman did manage to keep most of them up in the air by swatting at them and shouting, but then two dived over behind him.

Like a pair of shooting stars, the ivy leaf and the fig leaf shot downward to two of the cradles. Each poised for a moment over a yelling baby and then softly descended into the baby's wide-open bawling mouth. And were gone. A look of acute surprise crossed the face of each baby. Then they were yelling louder than ever with their faces screwed up and their short arms batting the air. It must feel very strange, Cat thought, suddenly to find you had two souls, but he could not see that it did any harm. And it was the perfect place to hide from Master Spiderman.

He nudged Tonino. "I think we'd better help them."

Tonino nodded. They set off down the ward just as things began to get difficult. Master Spiderman was speeding this way and that, scooping at darting souls, and most of the new mothers, tired as they were, were beginning to sit up and object. They could not seem to see the souls, but they could see Master Spiderman.

"What do you think you're doing?" several ladies demanded.

Another said, "I'm not letting that madman near my baby!" She picked her howling baby out of its cradle, just as the fluttering maple leaf soul was poised above it, and hugged it to her chest. The maple leaf was forced to swoop on to the next cradle, where Master Spiderman's butterfly net scooped at it and missed.

"He's a lunatic," said the mother in the next bed. "Ring the bell for help."

"I already did," said a mother in the bed opposite. "I rang twice now."

"It's too bad!" several mothers said. And several more shouted at Master Spiderman to get out or they would have the law on him.

Meanwhile, soul after soul darted away from Master Spiderman and vanished into babies. By this time, only two were left, the oldest and the newest. The oldest leaf was still stunted, though it seemed to have grown a little, but it was evidently bewildered and weak. All its efforts to get into babies were timid and slow, and whenever Master Spiderman's butterfly net swept towards it, all it seemed able to do was to flutter up towards the ceiling again, where the newest and biggest leaf-shape hovered, perhaps trying to tell the old leaf what to do.

The old soul timorously descended again as Cat and Tonino set off to help it. Master Spiderman pelted back to catch it. But he skidded to a stop when the ward doors clapped open and an awesome voice asked, "And what, pray, is the meaning of this?"

It was the Mother Superior. It did not take the hugeness of her starched headdress, the severity of her dark blue habit, the large silver cross hanging from her waist, or even her six feet of height, to tell you who and what she was. It was obvious. Such was the power of her personality that, as she advanced down the ward, nearly all the babies stopped crying.

The big soul that had been Gabriel de Witt hastily plunged from near the ceiling and was just in time to vanish into the only baby still crying. The mothers who were sitting up all hurriedly lay down again and the one who had picked her baby up guiltily popped it back into its cradle and lay down too. Cat and Tonino, feeling as guilty as the rest, stood still and tried to look as if they were visiting a new little brother or sister. Master Spiderman's flat mouth hung open as if the

Mother Superior had cast a spell on him. But Cat did not think it was magic. As the Mother Superior's cold eye passed over him, he knew it was pure personality. He wanted to sink into the floor.

"I do not," said the Mother Superior to Master Spiderman, "wish to know what you are doing here, my good man. I want you simply to take your butterfly net and your filthy street urchins, and leave. Now."

"Very good, ma'am." Master Spiderman cringed. His hairy monkey face twisted with guilt. For an instant, it seemed as if he was going to do as he was told and go away. But the stunted and bewildered old soul, which had been hovering miserably up near the ceiling, suddenly decided that the Mother Superior was the one to keep it safe. It came down in a fluttering spiral and landed on her great white headdress, where it nestled, frail and quivering, upon the highest starched point. Master Spiderman stared at it urgently, with round monkey eyes.

"Off you go," said the Mother Superior, "my good man."

Master Spiderman's face bunched up. "I'll have this one at least," Cat heard him mutter. He made one of his throwing gestures. "Freeze," he said.

The Mother Superior promptly became as stiff and still as a statue. Most of the babies started to cry again.

"Good," said Master Spiderman. "I never did hold with nuns. Nasty religious creatures." He stood on tiptoe to swat the roosting old soul into his net. But the Mother Superior's headdress was just too high for him. It flapped and rattled as he hit it, and the Mother Superior herself swayed about, and the soul, instead of being swatted into the net, was shot off sideways into the cradle that contained the twins. Both were bawling just then.

Cat saw the soul dive thankfully, but he did not see which twin got it, because Master Spiderman pushed him angrily aside and tried to unhook the cradle from the bed. "I'll have this one at least!" he cried out. "I'll start all over again, but I'll have *one*!"

"You will *not*!" said the mother of the twins. She climbed out of bed and advanced on Master Spiderman. She was enormous. She had huge arms that looked as if they had ploughed and reaped fields, made dough and pounded washing clean, until they were stronger than the arms of most men. The rest of her was in a vast white nightgown with a frill round its neck and, on top of the frill, was a surprisingly pretty and very determined face.

Cat took one look at her and respectfully handed her his butterfly net as she marched past him. She gave him a nod of thanks and absently turned it back to front, with the net near her hand. "Let go that cradle," she said, "or I shall make you very sorry."

Master Spiderman hastily hooked the cradle on to the bed again and backed away. "Let's be reasonable here, madam," he said in his most oily and placating manner. "You have two fine babies there. Suppose I were to give you a gold piece for the pair of them."

"I never," said the huge lady, "heard anything so disgusting in my life!" And she swung the shaft of the butterfly net with both hands.

Master Spiderman had just time to yell. "*Two* gold pieces then!" before the handle of the net met his head with a whistling *crack*. His hat came off, revealing his wispy brown scalp, and he tottered sideways, shrieking. Tottered some more and fell against the Mother Superior. Cat and Tonino were just in time to hold her upright by leaning against her as Master Spiderman slid howling down the front of her.

And as he slid, his bare head hit the silver cross hanging from the Mother Superior's waist. There was a strange crackling sound, followed by a strong smell. Master Spiderman jerked all over and hit the floor with an empty sort of flop. Cat found himself staring down at an old brown dead thing, that was so dried out and so withered that it might have been a mummified monkey. It looked as if it had died centuries before.

Cat's first act was to look anxiously around for any sign of Master Spiderman's soul. He did not want that getting into a baby. But it seemed almost as if any soul Master Spiderman had had was gone long ago. He could see and feel nothing of it. Then he looked down at the brown mummified thing again and thought, shuddering, If that's an evil enchanter, I don't want to be anything like *that*! At which point, he found he remembered who he was and that he was an enchanter too. And he was suddenly so engulfed in feelings and memories that he could not move.

Around him, the babies were all crying at full strength and most of their mothers were cheering. The mother of the twins was sitting on her bed saying she felt rather queer.

"I'm not surprised!" said the Mother Superior. "You did very well, my dear. A good flush hit – one of the best I've ever seen."

On the other side of the Mother Superior, Tonino was doing what Cat realised he should have been doing hours ago, and shouting at the top of his strong, clear voice. "Chrestomanci! Chrestomanci, come here quickly!"

There was a blat of warm moving air, like a train passing, combined with a strange spicy smell from another universe entirely, and Chrestomanci was standing in the ward, almost face to face with Mother Superior.

The effect was extremely odd. The Conclave of Mages seemed to require Chrestomanci to wear a skinny thigh-length white tunic above enormously baggy black trousers. It made him look even taller than the Mother Superior, and a great deal thinner.

"Ah, Mother Jannissary," he said. "Good evening. We met last year, I believe."

"At the canonical conference, and my name is Mother Justinia," the Mother Superior replied. "I am extremely glad to see you, Sir Christopher. We seem to have a spot of bother here."

"So I see," said Chrestomanci. He looked down at the remains of Master Spiderman and then across at Cat and Tonino. After that, his gaze travelled round the ward, the howling babies and the staring mothers, and he began to get his most bewildered look. "It seems a little late in the day for hospital visiting," he said. "Perhaps someone will tell me why we are all here." His brow creased and he made a little gesture, at which all the babies stopped crying and fell peacefully asleep. "That's better," he said. "Tonino, you explain."

Tonino told it, clearly and well. There were several occasions when Cat might have interrupted with some further explanations, but he scarcely said anything, because he was so ashamed. It was not just that he, a nine-lifed enchanter, had let Master Spiderman cast a spell on him to make him forget what he was – and he knew he should have noticed the spell: it must have been inside that old hackney cab – but the fact that he, Cat, had been so busy resenting Tonino that he had nearly got both of them killed.

It made him feel worse that Tonino kept saying that Cat had behaved well, and that Cat had been managing to work magic in spite of Master Spiderman's spells. Cat did not think either of these things were true. The most he could say for himself was he was glad he had been sorry for the trapped souls, enough to help rescue them. And he supposed he was glad to find he liked Tonino after all. Tonino had been so calm and sturdy through it all – the perfect companion. And he suspected that Tonino's back-up magic had done twice as much as his own.

"So Gabriel de Witt is dead," Chrestomanci said sadly.

"Not really," Tonino said, gesturing round at the sleeping babies. "He is here somewhere."

"Ah yes, but I imagine he – or she – doesn't know who he is now," Chrestomanci answered. He sighed. "So Neville Spiderman was hiding out in a time-bubble, collecting the souls of all the Chrestomancis, was he? And probably killing apprentices to prolong his own life while he waited. It was lucky he kidnapped the two of you. We'd never have caught him without that. But now we have, I think we'd better get rid of what's left of him – it looks infectious to me. How old is this hospital?" he asked the Mother Superior.

"About seventy years old," she replied, rather surprised.

"And what was here before it was built, do you know?" Chrestomanci asked.

She shrugged, rattling her headdress. "Just green fields, I think."

"Good," said Chrestomanci. "Then I can send him back in time without moving him. It's a bit hard on the person who falls over him in the field, but it fits with what I remember. He was supposed to have been found dead in a ditch somewhere near Dulwich. Will everyone please stand back?"

Cat, Tonino and Mother Justinia all backed away a pace. Before they had quite finished moving, a blue glow appeared round the monkey-like thing on the floor and Neville Spiderman was gone. This was followed by a rapidly evaporating puddle with a strong smell of hospital.

"Disinfectant," Chrestomanci explained. "Now, we have eight souls to account for still. Cat, can you remember which babies they all went to?"

Cat was more ashamed than ever. The babies all looked alike to him. And it had all been so confusing, with souls darting in all directions. "I've no idea," he confessed. "One of the twins, but I don't know which. And that's all."

"They all went everywhere," Tonino explained. "Won't their mothers know?"

"Most people," said Chrestomanci, "can't see souls. It takes magic. Oh well. We'll have to do it the hard way."

He turned round and snapped his fingers. The young man who acted as Chrestomanci's secretary jumped into existence further up the ward. He was obviously not used to this kind of summons. He was in the middle of tying a spotted bow tie and almost dropped it. Cat could see him staring round at the mothers, the babies and the Mother Superior, and then at the filthy and dishevelled boys, and trying to look as if he saw such things every day.

"Tom," Chrestomanci said to him, "be a good fellow and go round and get the names and addresses of all the mothers and every baby here, will you?"

"Certainly, sir," Tom said, trying to look efficient and understanding.

Some of the mothers looked indignant at this, and Mother Justinia said, "Is that really necessary? We like to be confidential here."

"Absolutely necessary," Chrestomanci said. He raised his voice so that all the mothers could hear him. "Some of your babies are going to grow up with very powerful magic. They might have strange memories, too, which could frighten both you and them. We want to be able to help them if this happens. We also want to educate them properly in the use of their magic. But, since none of us know *which* children are going to have these gifts, we are going to have to keep track of you all. So we are going to give each baby here a government grant of five hundred pounds a year until he or she is eighteen. Does this made you feel better about it?"

"You mean they get the money if they have magic or not?" somebody asked.

"Exactly," said Chrestomanci. "Of course they only get the grant when they come to Chrestomanci Castle once a year for magical testing."

"Mine might have magic anyway," someone else murmured. "My mother's father—"

The twins' mother said, "Well, I'm taking the money. I was at my wits' end how to give them all they need. I wasn't reckoning on twins. Thank you, sir."

"My pleasure, madam," Chrestomanci said, bowing to her. "Tom will give you any further details." Tom, who had just conjured himself a notebook and a pen, looked pleading and alarmed at this. Chrestomanci ignored him. "He can cope," he said to Cat. "That's what he's paid for. You and Tonino look as if you need a bath and a square meal. Let's take you both home."

"But—" said Cat.

"But what?" asked Chrestomanci.

Cat did not know how to put the shame he felt. He was fairly sure he had been starting to turn into someone like Neville Spiderman, but he did not dare tell Chrestomanci that. "I don't deserve anything," he said.

"No more than those twins deserve five hundred pounds a year each," Chrestomanci said cheerfully. "I don't know what's biting you, Cat, but it seems to me that you've managed rather well in a dangerous situation without thinking you can rely on magic to help you. Think about it."

Beside Cat, Tonino exclaimed. Cat looked up from the floor to find they were in the grand central hall of Chrestomanci Castle, standing in the five pointed star under the chandelier. Millie was rushing down the marble stairs to meet them.

"Oh, you *found* them!" she called out. "I've been so

worried. Mordecai telephoned to say he put them in a cab which disappeared at the end of the street. He was terribly upset. And Gabriel de Witt died this evening, did you hear?"

"After a fashion," Chrestomanci said. "In one way, Gabriel's still very much with us." He looked from Millie to Cat and Tonino. "Dear, dear. Everyone looks exhausted. I tell you what. I can borrow a villa in the South of France once the measles have abated – with a swimming pool. Tonino can go on to Italy from there. Would you like that, Tonino?"

"Yes, but I cannot swim," Tonino said.

"Neither can I," Cat said. "But we can both learn."

Tonino beamed at him and Cat was glad to discover he still liked Tonino, rather a lot.

Chrestomanci

Charmed Life

Everybody says that Gwendolyn
Chant is a gifted witch with
astonishing powers, so it suits
her enormously when she is
taken to live in Chrestomanci
Castle. Her brother Eric (better
known as Cat) is not so keen.
However, life with the great
enchanter is not what either of
them expects!

Also available on tape,
read by Tom Baker

Book isbn: 0 00 675515 1
Tape isbn: 0 00 710653 X

Chrestomanci

The Magicians of Caprona

Casa Montana and Casa Petrocchi look after the magical business in Caprona, watched over by its magnificent guardian statue, the Angel. The families have been feuding for years, so when young Tonino Montana and Angelica Petrocchi disappear, each naturally blame the other. Or is Caprona in the grip of a darker enemy?

Also available on tape,
read by Nickolas Grace

Book isbn: 0 00 675516 X
Tape isbn: 0 00 710654 8

Chrestomanci

Chrestomanci

Witch Week

When a note appears between two of the homework books Mr Crossley is marking, he is very upset. It says: SOMEONE IN THIS CLASS IS A WITCH. The most awful thing is, the note might be true – for Larwood House is a school for witch-orphans! The last thing they need is a visit from the Divisional Inquisitor…

Also available on tape,
read by Ursula Jones

Book isbn: 0 00 675517 8
Tape isbn: 0 00 710655 6

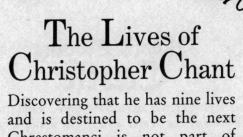

The Lives of Christopher Chant

Discovering that he has nine lives and is destined to be the next Chrestomanci is not part of Christopher's plans for the future: he'd much rather play cricket and wander around his secret dream worlds. But he soon finds that destiny is difficult to avoid, and that having more than the usual number of lives is pretty inconvenient – especially when you lose them as easily as he does!

Also available on tape,
read by Samuel West

Book isbn: 0 00 675518 6
Tape isbn: 0 00 710656 4

Mixed Magics

Available on tape in September 2002...

Howl's Moving Castle

When Sophie Hatter attracts the unwelcome attention of the Witch of the Waste and is put under a curse, she travels to one place where she might get help – the moving castle which hovers on the nearby hills. But the castle belongs to dreaded Wizard Howl whose appetite is satisfied only by the hearts of young girls...

Also available on tape, read by John Sessions

Book isbn: 0 00 675523 2
Tape isbn: 0 00 712222 5

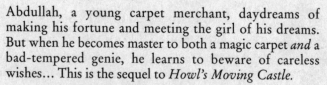

Castle in the Air

Abdullah, a young carpet merchant, daydreams of making his fortune and meeting the girl of his dreams. But when he becomes master to both a magic carpet *and* a bad-tempered genie, he learns to beware of careless wishes... This is the sequel to *Howl's Moving Castle*.

Also available on tape, read by John Sessions

Book isbn: 0 00 675530 5
Tape isbn: 0 00 712223 3

Black Maria

Great Aunt Maria seems like a cuddly old lady, all chit-chat and lace doilies and unadulterated **NICE**ness! But Mig and her family soon learn that Aunt Maria rules Cranbury-on-Sea with a rod of sweetness that's tougher than iron and deadlier than poison. Is Aunt Maria a witch? Maybe the ghost in the bedroom holds the key…?

Also available on tape, read by Ursula Jones

Book isbn: 0 00 675528 3
Tape isbn: 0 00 711387 0

Archer's Goon

When the Goon turns up demanding "Archer's two thousand", life turns upside-down. As Howard desperately tries to get to the bottom of this peculiar demand, he discovers that the town is run by seven crazy wizards (not all of whom live in the present!) and someone is trying to take over the world!

Also available on tape, read by Miriam Margolyes

Book isbn: 0 00 675527 5
Tape isbn: 0 00 713479 7

Wilkins' Tooth

Own Back Limited seemed like a good idea at the time.
After all Frank and Jess need the money and a revenge
business should be the ideal way to earn it. But good ideas
like revenge tend to go horribly wrong and soon they find
themselves in deep trouble with Buster Knell's gang, two
strange little girls – even poor old Biddy Iremonger.

isbn: 0 00 712965 3

power
of
three

Gair, Ayna and Ceri live on the moor. Ayna and Ceri have
special powers, but Gair is just ordinary and feels he must
be a great disappointment to everyone. For the moor
people are under a curse, and special powers are
desperately needed to keep it at bay. Their enemies, the
Dorig, are a constant threat, and the Giants are behaving
strangely too. Their only hope is to try and lift the curse...

isbn: 0 00 711370 6

THE
HOMEWARD
BOUNDERS

When Jamie unwittingly discovers the scary, dark-cloaked
Them playing games with human's lives, he is cast out to
the boundaries of the worlds. Clinging to Their promise
that if he can get Home he is free, he becomes the
unwilling Random Factor in an endless game of chance.

isbn: 0 00 675525 9

EIGHT DAYS
OF LUKE

"Just kindle a flame and I'll be with you," says Luke.
David thinks he's joking, but certainly, whenever he
strikes a match, Luke appears immediately. But David's
new friend seems to have some extraordinary friends
and relations, and some very dark secrets. And when
David enters into a bargain with the mysterious one-
eyed Mr Wedding, life gets very hot indeed!

isbn: 0 00 675521 6

If you enjoyed this book why not come back to Ottakar's and try another of these fantastic books by Diana Wynne Jones?

Charmed Life

"Gwendolyn Chant, a gifted witch, and her brother Eric are taken to live at Chrestomanci Castle, with unexpected results for both of them. A wonderful read for fans of the Harry Potter books."
Rosemary (Launch Pad, Meadowhall)

The Magicians of Caprona

For centuries two feuding families, the Montana and the Petrocchi, have prepared the magic of Caprona, watched over by a guardian statue, the Angel. When the spells start to go wrong the families turn on each other... A must read for Chrestomanci fans, and anyone who enjoys a good magical adventure mystery.
Gina (Ottakar's, Basildon)

Witch Week

"In a world where magic is forbidden, the appearance of a note stating "Someone in this class is a witch" can only spell trouble! But it could be any one of the pupils in class 2Y, for Larwood House is a school for witch-orphans!"
Karen (Ottakar's, Carlisle)

OTTAKAR'S